How The Tooth Fairy Got Her Job

Written by Gilson Henry　　**Illustrated by Joyce Eide**

Purple Turtle Books, Inc.

Imaginative Stories For Imaginative Children

Once upon a fairy tale
So many years ago,
There lived a fairy princess,
Her name I'm sure you know.

In her far off kingdom,
The princess was so blue.
What job was hers in fairy land?
Whatever could she do?

All her friends were busy,
Each with a job to do.
She wanted to be like them
So she'd be helping too.

But where, oh where was her place?
She truly longed to know.
And what, oh what could she do,
A job she needed so.

She loved the Strawberry Fairy
With her red and curly hair.
When those berries were growing,
The fairy was always there.

There was the Fairy of Rainbows,
Painting colors in the sky.
Seeing that gardens were watered
When a rain cloud would pass by.

There was the Fairy of Peacocks,
How full of color was she.
Making sure proud peacocks
Were the brightest sight to see.

One night she saw a little girl,
Who in thought had bowed her head.
In her tiny hand a tooth was held,
And this is what she said.

"I wish this tooth I have lost,
So shiny and so white,
Could go up high into the sky,
Be a little twinkling light."

The Princess now was happy
For she could plainly see,
She would gather those lost teeth,
And the Tooth Fairy she would be.

Aren't you glad the princess,
Her faith she never lost.
To become someone better
Was worth the time it cost.

The fairy comes at night time
From out of skies above.
She takes the tooth so softly
And leaves a coin of love.

When all the teeth she's gathered,
She flies up very high,
Finds a place for every one,
Adding starlight to the sky.

When you see the stars at night,
If you've lost a tooth or two,
You may find one up there,
The one that winks at you.

When you wish upon a star,
To be bigger than you are.
You will find it's up to you,
To make your wish come true.

It's up to you to do your best
In all things that you do,
To reach your goal, make it yours,
To have your dream come true.